GOOD NEWS NELSON

Story by Jodi Moore

Illustrated by Brendan Flannelly-King

Story Pie Press | Virginia

**Publisher's Cataloging-in-Publication
(Provided by Quality Books, Inc.)**

Moore, Jodi.
      Good news Nelson / by Jodi Moore ; illustrated by
Brendan Flannelly-King.
      p. cm.
      SUMMARY: Nelson, a newspaper delivery boy,
discovers "news" of 100 abandoned cats and devises
a plan to save them all, while helping the local animal
shelter.
      Audience: Ages 4-9.
      LCCN 2012945212
      ISBN-13: 978-0-9842178-3-0 (hardcover)
      ISBN-10: 0-9842178-3-5 (hardcover)
      ISBN-13: 978-0-9842178-4-7 (pbk.)
      ISBN-10: 0-9842178-4-3 (pbk.)

      1. Paperboys--Juvenile fiction. 2. Older women--
Juvenile fiction. 3. Cats--Juvenile fiction.
[1. Paperboys--Fiction. 2. Older women--Fiction.
3.Cats--Fiction.]   I. Flannelly-King, Brendan, ill. II. Title.

PZ7.M78617Goo 2012   [E]
                 QBI12-600177

Published by Story Pie Press
Copyright 2012 Story Pie Press, LLC
All rights reserved.
To request permission to reproduce selections from this
book, email publisher@storypiepress.com.

www.storypiepress.com

Edited by Mary Rand Hess

Book design by Amber Leberman

The text of this book is set in Olivetti Typewriter.
Other typefaces used are Ultinoid and Myriad Pro.

The illustrations are done in
acrylic, colored pencil and collage.

Printed in the United States of America

With love to my family: my parents, my siblings Neil and Staci (the "real" Mrs. Welsh), my husband Larry and our kids, Steve, Alex and Jess...for showing me everything is possible through love, passion and compassion.

For our beloved Little One. Miss you, angel kitty. Special love and gratitude extended to Mary Rand Hess and Shari Dash Greenspan for believing in NELSON (and in me) since his conception, and for helping to deliver "my baby" into the world.

~ J. M.

To Anna and Eamon and also to Ged (RIP).

~ B. F. K.

When Nelson delivers newspapers,
he always calls, "Good morning!" to
his neighbors.

"What's the good news, Nelson?" they reply.

But not cranky, old Mrs. Snodberry. She waits, foot tapping,
at the end of the block on her creaky, old porch, clutching
her crumpled, old cat.

When Nelson says, "Good morning," she says, "Bah! More bad news." She adjusts her glasses pinched low on her crinkly, old nose and scans the headlines.

"Bah! High prices!"

"Bah! People fighting!"

"Bah! Rotten weather!"

Then, with the cat tucked under one arm, and her paper under the other, she waddles inside her house. "Bah!" Nelson hears as the screen door bangs shut.

Each morning it's the same. Until this Monday morning. When it's different.

Oh, there waits cranky, old Mrs. Snodberry on her creaky, old porch with her crumpled, old cat. She grumbles her usual "Bah!" But when she scans the headlines, her lips suck in a big breath. Behind her thick glasses, her eyes grow wide and her mouth sags.

"Oh, Precious," Mrs. Snodberry says to her cat. "Bad, bad news. One hundred kitties found abandoned in an old house. People just don't care anymore."

"People care," Nelson starts to say, but Mrs. Snodberry is already waddling inside, clutching her newspaper in one hand and Precious in the other. "I care!"

"Bah!" he hears as the screen door bangs shut.

Maybe caring isn't enough, Nelson thinks as he walks home. Maybe I can help.

But what can I do?

"Mom," Nelson asks when he reaches his house. "Can we adopt 100 cats?"

Mom has read the article, too. "I'm afraid not," she says. "But maybe we can help in some other way. Let's ask at the animal rescue shelter."

Mrs. Welsh runs the shelter. She is bursting with ideas. "Of course we want good homes for the kitties, but in the meantime, we need donations of cat food," she says. "And newspapers, to line the cages."

Newspapers?

A thought begins to grow in Nelson's head.

A thought that becomes a plan.

On Tuesday, Nelson goes door-to-door delivering his newspapers. But instead of just leaving the paper, Nelson rings the bell.

"What's the good news, Nelson?" neighbors say as they answer the door.

"Do you still have yesterday's paper?"

He tells them about the homeless cats and the shelter's need for newspapers.

"Each day, when I bring your new paper, I'll take your old one to the shelter for you."

Even Mrs.
Snodberry waddles
inside to get her
old papers for him.
For once, she doesn't
say, "Bah." Instead,
she wheels out a
rickety wagon.

"Figured this might help cart the extra papers."

Before Nelson can thank her, she hobbles inside.

Nelson arrives at the shelter to find mounds of purring fluff everywhere: inside carriers, perched on chairs, atop the bookshelf and desk, tumbling on the floor...he's knee deep in feline fuzzies galore!

Mrs. Welsh is grateful, but worried. "We have so many cats, we've run out of room. We can't take in any more animals until we find homes for the ones we have."

Two kittens curl around Nelson's legs. "If only people could see them..." As his smile grows, so does an idea! Nelson snaps a picture with his phone. "I've got news to share!"

On Wednesday, Nelson delivers his papers with a special flyer:

Mrs. Snodberry shows the picture to Precious. "Remember when you were that little?" She dabs watery eyes before waddling inside.

By Thursday, Nelson can barely pull his wagon! Mrs. Welsh beams. Now there's plenty of paper for the cages, and people are lining up to adopt the cats, all thanks to Nelson's campaign.

"I don't know what's been more helpful," she says. "Having you deliver the good news, Nelson, or having you pick it back up again!"

All week, Nelson delivers his papers.
All week, he picks up the old ones.

But on Friday, when Nelson gets to the
end of the block, there is no Mrs. Snodberry
waiting on her porch. When he rings her bell, no
one answers. Not even Precious.

That's odd, Nelson thinks and leaves a newspaper on
Mrs. Snodberry's doormat.

Where could she be? Nelson wonders as he walks home.

"Nelson, you have a visitor," Mom announces. Mrs. Snodberry is in his own living room, clutching her cat and having tea with Mom!

Mrs. Snodberry slowly rises. Behind thick glasses, her eyes glisten. "You turned bad news into good news, Nelson, because you care. Thank you."

She shuffles over to a large cardboard box, reaches in and lifts out two kittens.

"Just adopted 'em," she says. "One's mine. Figured it was time Precious had a new friend."

Her wrinkly face breaks into a smile.

"The other one is for you."

Nelson cuddles the kitten. "For me? Like, a present?"

"Yes, Nelson. Figured it was time I had a new friend, too."

Grinning at each other and clutching their cats, the two friends waddle back to Mrs. Snodberry's porch together. After all, Nelson hasn't picked up her old paper yet.

The end.